DISNEY

HANNAH MONTANA

Wishful Thinking

Based on the s   en

rt One is based on the   las Lieblein

Part Two is based o   oiduss

DISNEY CHANNEL

DISNEY PRESS

New York

PART ONE

Chapter One

Hannah Montana's strong, clear voice filled the arena. She was bringing another amazing concert to a close with one of her favorite songs, "Old Blue Jeans." The band was on fire, and the backup dancers swirled around Hannah. The audience cheered loudly as she sang the last note of the song. She waved good-bye to her fans before dashing backstage and into her dressing room.

"Hannah, you rock! I can't believe you did three encores!" Lola Luftnagle said loudly. She closed the dressing-room door to make sure they were alone. Then her tone changed to one of irritation. "I can't believe you did three encores. You know we have a science project due Monday. What is wrong with you?"

Hannah Montana wasn't just a teen superstar, she was also a regular high-school girl named Miley Stewart. Miley loved being Hannah Montana when she was onstage or in the recording studio. Offstage, she traded in her blond wig and pop-star clothes for a normal life as brown-haired teenager Miley Stewart. And Miley's life included homework and tests.

Together, Miley, her family, and her friends, Oliver Oken and Lilly Truscott, kept Hannah Montana's true identity a secret. That way Miley could know for sure that people liked her for who she was and not just because she was a famous pop star. And Lola Luftnagle was really Miley's friend Lilly, disguised in a colorful wig and a funky outfit.

Most of the time Miley liked living a secret, double life. She got to be a pop star and a regular girl. To her, it was the best of both worlds. It also meant that unlike most pop stars, she had to deal with things like science projects and math tests.

"Oh. Oh, okay," Miley said. "Let's leave this boring rock-star life behind and get back to the glamorous world of earthworm larvae."

At that moment, Hannah Montana's bodyguard, Roxy, poked her head into the dressing room. "You decent, girl?" she asked. "I've got your squeaky little friend out here—"

"I've told you, it's a nasal condition," Traci Van Horne snapped at Roxy as she stepped into the room. Then she turned to Miley. "And Hannah, I brought someone who wants to meet you." Traci was not in on Miley's secret.

"No way," Lilly said quietly to Miley. "We're already late. I promised our larvae we'd be home by ten."

"Okay, fine," Miley whispered. "I'll get rid of whoever it is and—"

Just then, Jesse McCartney walked into the room. "Hi, I'm Jesse," he said.

Every thought Miley had flew out of her head. She couldn't believe it—supercute, supertalented Jesse McCartney was in her dressing room!

"Eeeeeep!" Lilly instantly let out a high-pitched squeal.

"Oh, my gosh," Miley babbled, bouncing up and down. "It's Jesse McCartney! I love you!" She realized she sounded just as excited as some of her Hannah Montana fans. She was supposed to be used to meeting other celebrities. Miley tried to take it down a notch. "I mean, I'm a big fan. *Big* fan!"

Jesse smiled. "Listen, tonight *I'm* the fan. You did a great job." He extended his hand to Lilly. "And you are?" he asked.

Lilly squealed again as she shook his hand. *"Eeeeep."*

"Nice to meet you . . . *Eeeeep,*" Jesse said with a smile. "Listen, Hannah, a bunch of my friends and I are going to the Dragon Room tonight. You want to come?"

"Yes!" Miley did not have to think about that at all.

"No!" Lilly said at the same time, remembering their earthworm project.

"No?" Miley asked, confused.

"Yes!" Lilly answered.

"Excuse us," Miley said to Jesse. She pulled Lilly aside. She couldn't believe her best friend had embarrassed her like that in front of Jesse McCartney. "What are you doing?" she whispered.

"Our science project," Lilly reminded her.

"Oh, right," Miley said, remembering. "Oh, I've got the fix: you do all the work, and *I'll* go out with Jesse. Toodles!" she said happily.

Lilly pulled her back. "I've got a better idea. You give me the Hannah wig, and I'll go out with Jesse."

"I don't think he speaks *'Eeeep!'*" Miley said sarcastically.

Jesse could tell the girls were arguing, but he didn't know what the problem was.

"Listen, ladies, if tonight isn't a good night, then why don't we do it tomorrow?" he suggested.

Miley was relieved. She could do her science project and still hang out with Jesse. "That would be absolutely—"

"Math test," Lilly whispered in Miley's ear.

"—impossible," Miley said. "How about Tuesday?"

"Yearbook committee," Lilly whispered.

"—of next week?" Miley finished.

"Homecoming float," Lilly whispered in her ear again.

"Which I just realized is no good either," Miley said awkwardly. There was no way she could admit she had homework without telling Jesse about her double life. He knew her only as Hannah Montana. Pop stars didn't have school commitments.

"Busy, busy, busy bee. Yep, that's me," she said. "Why don't I just text you?"

"No thanks," Jesse replied. "Getting rejected in person is enough. I don't need to have it in writing." After so many excuses, he was sure Hannah didn't want to hang out with him.

Miley tried to think of something to say, but all she could do was watch him leave.

Later that evening, Miley sat on the porch of her Malibu beach house with Lilly. They were surrounded by science texts, notebooks, and a terrarium filled with dirt and earthworms. This was *so* not the glamorous life of a pop star, Miley thought as she watched a worm wiggle between her fingers.

"This stinks!" she said.

Lilly shrugged. "Of course they stink.

They live in their own poop."

"Not the worms! My life. I can't believe I gave up Jesse McCartney for a slimy piece of fish bait," Miley complained.

Lilly gasped and took the worm from Miley. "She didn't really mean that, Ernie. She loves you," Lilly said to the worm, then placed it carefully back in the terrarium.

"If only I could have told Jesse the truth!" Miley said with a sigh. She stood up and leaned over the porch railing and gazed up at the night sky. "He would have understood about school stuff. But then I'd blow the secret."

Lilly joined her friend and gave her a sympathetic smile.

"This double life is so hard," Miley continued.

At that moment, a shooting star passed overhead.

"Oooh, look, a shooting star." Lilly closed her eyes. "I wish for an A on the project. What do you wish for?"

"Oh, man, I wish . . ." Miley stopped to think. "I wish there was no secret and I was just Hannah Montana all the time. It sure would make life a whole lot easier."

Miley and Lilly went back inside to finish their project. When it was done, Lilly headed home, and Miley went to bed.

The next morning when Miley woke up, she felt something soft under her cheek. She realized she was lying on a fur-covered pillow. She sat up and stretched with a yawn, then scratched her head. Her hair felt funny. It was perfectly smooth like her Hannah wig, instead of curly and tangled like the mess it was most mornings. She pulled her hair in front of her face and saw that it was blond, not brown. Had she fallen asleep in her Hannah wig?

Miley tugged on her blond hair. "*Ow!* What the—" She yanked, harder this time. But the wig wouldn't come off. It felt like she was pulling her own hair.

She jumped out of bed and ran over to her makeup table. As Miley gazed around, she realized that this wasn't her bedroom. Instead, it looked like a pop star's bedroom. The room was decorated with lots of fur, gold, and sparkly furnishings. Miley looked down at herself. Where were the T-shirt and pajama pants she normally slept in, she wondered. Miley would never wear the blue silk pajamas she had on—except on a Hannah Montana fashion shoot.

Miley grabbed a mirror and stared at herself. She almost dropped it in shock. Miley was gone! Hannah Montana had taken her place! "What is going on?" she yelled.

Suddenly her room was filled with lots of twinkling lights. Roxy appeared, dressed in a white outfit. "Your wish came true, girl," she said.

"Whoa!" Miley's jaw dropped. Had Roxy just appeared out of a bunch of lights? Miley was confused, not to mention a little frightened.

"You didn't want to be Miley. Well, now you're all Hannah, *aaaallll* the time!" Roxy said.

Miley looked in the mirror again. Hannah's reflection looked back at her. What was going on, Miley wondered. Had her wish really come true?

Chapter Two

Once she'd had a second to think things over, Miley decided this must be a trick. She glared at Roxy. Hannah's bodyguard must have redecorated her bedroom and somehow glued the wig on her head while Miley slept. It had to be a practical joke, but it was definitely not funny.

"What are you talking about?" Miley asked.

"You wished for one life, and you got it,"

Roxy explained. "In this world, Miley Stewart never existed."

"Ha, ha, very funny, Roxy," Miley said. She crossed her arms over her chest.

"Oh, I'm not Roxy. I'm an angel. I'm only taking the shape of Roxy to make you more comfortable." She flexed her muscled arms. "And I'm loving it!"

Now Miley got it—Roxy had lost her mind. "*Ooookay*," Miley said slowly. "How about you just wait here while I get some very nice men with a very big net."

"Oh, you don't believe me? Well, if I weren't an angel, could I do this?" Roxy waved her hands and floated off the ground! Little white wings fluttered on the back of each of her sneakers. "Check out my fly kicks," Roxy continued. "And I do mean *fly* kicks."

"No, no, no," Miley said, watching Roxy

gently land. "This can *not* be happening."

"Oh, it's already happened. You wished upon a star, and now Hannah Montana is who you are," Roxy said. Then she snapped her fingers. Suddenly, they were both surrounded by twinkling stars, and Hannah's bedroom disappeared.

When the twinkling stars faded away, Miley and Roxy were in the Stewarts' Malibu living room. Miley looked around in shock. The room had been transformed. There was absolutely no trace of the Stewarts—everything was about Hannah Montana. There were gold records on the walls, Hannah concert posters, and Hannah memorabilia items all over the room. Her family's familiar, comfortable furniture had been replaced with hip new tables and chairs.

"Wow," Miley said.

"Nice crib, huh?" Roxy asked.

"Look at this place," Miley said. "It's *soooo* pop star. I mean, the twinkling lights, the leather couch, and that awesome chandelier." She pointed to a collection of white branches adorned with lights. "Madonna has one just like it."

Roxy shook her head. "Not anymore."

"I love this!" Miley shouted excitedly. Her house was awesome.

"You ain't seen nothing yet," Roxy promised.

A chef walked into the room carrying a cake in an H and M shape. "Your favorite breakfast cake, Mademoiselle Montana," he said with a French accent.

Miley couldn't believe it. She got to eat cake for breakfast? Her father wouldn't even put chocolate chips in their pancakes! "Triple Dutch chocolate?" Miley asked.

"With the fudge-ripple middle," the chef answered.

This was getting better and better. "I *really* love this," Miley said.

"I will put it next to the hot tub," the chef said, heading toward the porch, "so you can chill out while you pig out."

"*Merci, Pierre! C'est très, très bien.*" Miley realized she knew the chef's name, even though she had never seen him before. "I speak French!" she said to Roxy, surprised.

"You have a whole different life," Roxy explained. "You lived in France, you own polo ponies, and you're a black belt in jujitsu, which came in handy when you fought that tiger on *Circus with the Stars*." Roxy growled for effect.

"I fought a tiger? I am so cool!" Miley said.

Just then, Mr. Corelli, one of Miley's

high-school teachers, walked through the front door. He was wearing a bright blue jacket with a Hannah Montana logo. "Good morning, Hannah!"

"Mr. Corelli?" Miley replied in disbelief. "What are you doing here?"

"Homeschool teacher," Roxy whispered. "Hannah can't go to public school."

"Just came in early for a little chow," Mr. Corelli answered, patting his stomach. "You know how I love Pierre's *omelette du fromage*. By the way," he said, taking advantage of a teaching opportunity, "that's French for cheese omelet."

"I know!" Miley said, psyched by her ability to speak a foreign language.

She followed Mr. Corelli toward the kitchen.

"Oh, hey, Hannah, do you have that history report for me?" he asked.

"Um, history report. Right, well, um . . ." Miley stammered. History report? Had Hannah done it? Miley didn't know.

"No excuses, young lady," Mr. Corelli said sternly. "If you do not have that report . . ." He threw his arms up in the air. "Who cares? It's homeschooling *à la* Corelli."

Miley smiled. She could really get used to this.

"By the way, loving the team-Montana jacket." Mr. Corelli struck a pose. "Bling! Wore it to the salon yesterday. Got a free back wax."

Miley tried to block that mental picture and quickly brought the subject back to her schoolwork. "So, I don't have to worry about my assignments?" she asked.

"You don't have to worry about *anything*. You're Hannah Montana," Mr. Corelli said, pointing to a large portrait on the wall that made Hannah look like a superstar *and* a superhero.

"And I'm loving it!" Miley said. She jumped over the back of the couch and stretched out with a pillow in her lap.

"Yeah, life's pretty sweet when you're not dealing with all that Miley stuff," Roxy said.

"You got that right," Miley agreed. "No math test, no stinky earthworms . . ."

"And more time to spend with your *ma-an*," Roxy said, stretching the word out into two syllables.

"I've got a '*ma-an*'?" Miley said, imitating her.

"Not just *a* man. But *the* man." Roxy snapped her fingers, and Miley felt herself dissolve into a cloud of twinkling stars again.

❄ ❄ ❄

When the twinkling stars cleared, Miley was in a gondola in Venice. She was wearing a fabulous Hannah Montana outfit. Best of all, Jesse McCartney sat by her side.

A gondolier poled the boat through the water. He began to sing to the couple.

"Oh, *mamma mia*," Miley said, resting her head on Jesse's shoulder. She was stunned. Was this real? Was she really in Italy with Jesse McCartney? It had to be the most romantic thing that had ever happened to her.

"The perfect night with the perfect girl," Jesse said, gazing into her eyes.

The gondolier continued to sing.

"I'd sing it for you myself, but I need my lips for something else," Jesse said.

Was Jesse McCartney going to kiss her? Miley couldn't believe it. *"Eeeep!"* she squealed.

"You are so cute when you say *'eeeep'*,"
Jesse said with a grin.

Miley leaned in for her kiss. Just then,
Roxy came out of the water and pulled herself up using the side of the boat. She was
wearing a wet suit and a snorkel mask.
"Sorry, sugar, but my wings are getting all
soggy." She snapped her fingers.

Miley opened her eyes. Her lips were
still pursed for a kiss. But Venice and the
romantic gondola setting had disappeared.
She was back on the couch in her living
room, wearing Hannah's blue pajamas.
Miley lost her balance and fell forward into
a pillow.

That was *so* not how I expected it to go,
Miley thought.

Chapter Three

"Oh, man. You couldn't have given me one more minute?" Miley asked as she sat up.

Roxy sat on top of a white baby grand piano, still dressed in the wet suit she'd been wearing in Italy. She pulled the snorkel out of her mouth and spit water into a bowl. "Sorry, but the top of a gondola is romantic. The bottom? Nasty."

"I can't believe it," Miley said, standing

up. "All these years, I was so paranoid about my secret getting out. But, boy, was I wrong. This life is perfect."

Just then, a woman walked through the front door. She was wearing a ski outfit. She was gorgeous, but she had on too much makeup and her hair was teased into a high ponytail.

"Hannahkins!" The woman rushed over and hugged Miley. "How's my favorite little pop star?" she asked in a sugary-sweet voice.

"Great," Miley said. "And how's my favorite little . . ." She turned to Roxy for a hint.

"Stepmom," Roxy told her.

"Step — *what*?" Miley exclaimed.

"Candice was your first homeschool teacher," Roxy explained.

"And now she's my mom?" Miley asked.

"That must have been some parent-teacher conference."

"*Mmmm-hmmmm*," Roxy agreed.

Miley's dad walked through the front door wearing his own flashy ski outfit. Mr. Stewart's hair was in a ponytail, something Miley had never seen before, and he carried a snowboard and goggles.

"Hey, hey, darlin'. You missed some gnarly boarding," he said to Miley.

"'Gnarly boarding'?" Miley repeated. Was this really her father?

Mr. Stewart hadn't picked up on Miley's tone. "Totally! The next time we go to Switzerland you *soooo* gotta come with us. It was off the hook!"

"Radical," Candice agreed.

"But I'm back now, baby. Give me a hug." He threw his arms around Miley.

The hug felt different. It wasn't the soft,

cushy hug Miley remembered. "Whoa, have you been working out?" she asked, squeezing her father's arms.

He flexed his biceps. "Oh, I've *so* got to stay in shape to keep up with this little kitten," he said as he grinned at Candice.

Candice held up her hands and pretended they were cat claws, then meowed at Mr. Stewart. He meowed back. Then they both began giggling, and he chased her up the stairs.

Miley and Roxy watched them go. Miley felt nauseated.

"I got some *yakety-yak* coming back," Roxy said. "How about you?"

"Little bit," Miley agreed. She shook off the creepiness of the situation. Her dad was acting really different. And a stepmom? "But you know what? My dad's happy, and that's all that matters, right?"

Roxy nodded. "That's the spirit. Don't let a little bump in the road get you down."

Miley thought for a moment. "Speaking of little bumps, where's Jackson?"

"Oh, he doesn't live here anymore," Roxy answered.

Doesn't live here anymore? Miley had often wished her older brother would disappear, but the idea of him living elsewhere seemed strange.

Roxy snapped her fingers. Once again, Miley faded into thousands of twinkling stars.

When the sparkling lights cleared, Miley found herself standing on a sand dune. She was wearing fitted jeans, sunglasses, and a long, flowing scarf—Hannah Montana clothes. A moment later, Roxy appeared out of the sky and dropped behind the dune with a *thump*!

"Sometimes this teleporting stuff ain't easy," Roxy said with a groan. She brushed herself off and limped up the dune to stand next to Miley. "Oh, no, I dinged a wing."

Miley was about to sympathize when she heard a strange sound. Turning, she saw a guy who looked as if he hadn't had a haircut, a shave, or a bath in a very long time. His scraggly beard was almost to his waist. He was scanning the sand on the beach with a metal detector. The device made an unusual, high-pitched sound.

As the guy continued to scan the sand, the metal detector's static got louder.

"Oh, ho, ho!" the guy yelled. "I gotcha!"

As soon as Miley heard his voice, she recognized the person under all the dirt and hair. "Jackson?" she said in disbelief.

He didn't hear her. Jackson dived onto the sand and started digging with his hands. He found the piece of metal he had been looking for and held up his prize. "Eeeee, doggies! A quarter. I'm eatin' good tonight!"

Miley turned to Roxy, confused.

"Hannah Montana," Roxy answered. "He got tired of people pretending to be his friend just to get to you. So he dropped out and became a hermit."

Jackson walked past them.

"A *stinky* hermit," Roxy added as she wrinkled her nose.

Jackson turned his metal detector back on and continued to scan the sand. A boy stopped and watched him with a curious expression.

"Hey, what are you looking at? Git!

Git!" Jackson shouted in an unusually harsh-sounding voice.

"What happened to his voice?" Miley asked.

"Nothing. He just does that to scare people away," Roxy said.

"Jackson? Oh, Jackson?" Miley called, trying to get her brother's attention. Finally, Miley ran in front of him.

Jackson used the metal detector to scan his sister. The beeping got louder as the scanner got closer to her Hannah Montana jewelry.

"Sweet nuggets! I hit the mother lode!" Jackson shouted. Then he recognized his sister. "Oh, it's just the load," he said, sounding disappointed.

"Jackson, was being my brother really that bad?" Miley asked.

"Yes. Now git!" Jackson told her. "I got

my own life now. And me and my dolphin brothers and sisters don't care about no Hanny Montany."

In the ocean, a dolphin made a screeching noise.

"Except for Dave. He loves you," Jackson admitted.

The dolphin screeched again.

"Forget it, Dave," Jackson yelled. "You want an autograph, come up here and ask her yourself." He stormed off toward the water.

"Wow," Miley said to Roxy. "When he dropped out, he must've landed on his head."

She looked around and saw her old beach hangout, Rico's Surf Shop. Her friend Oliver Oken stood in front. But he looked different. His hair was slicked back. He wore sunglasses, a hat, and lots of gold chains.

"Yo, yo, yo. If you wanna be viewin' on what a pop star's doin', just slide me a five and watch the Hannah-house live," Oliver rapped.

"I cannot believe it. Oliver's selling peeks into my house. It's like he's turned into a . . . a . . ." Miley tried to think of the right word.

"A stretched-out version of *that*?" Roxy asked, pointing down the beach.

Miley turned to see Rico strutting up to the snack shop. He was wearing the same outfit as Oliver. The only difference was that he was about a foot and a half shorter than him.

Miley and her friends had never gotten along with Rico. Why was Oliver hanging out with him now?

"How we doing today, twice-my-size?" Rico asked Oliver.

"Makin' bacon, Mini Me," Oliver said as he pulled out a thick wad of cash.

"And you ain't fakin'," Rico said with a nod. "Time to do—"

"—a little shakin'!" the boys said at the same time. Then they started dancing badly.

Miley watched with a look of disgust on her face.

"And all this happened because . . ." Roxy prompted. She waited for Miley to finish the sentence.

"Because I was never Miley. I never went to regular school. I never met Oliver. I get it," she said. She didn't want to admit it, but maybe being Hannah Montana all the time wasn't the greatest thing in the world. Maybe Miley had been good for her friends. Her friends . . . Suddenly, she realized that she still hadn't seen her very *best* friend. "Angel, what happened to Lilly?" Miley asked.

Roxy pointed, and Miley saw Lilly walking across the beach with the two meanest and most popular girls in their class — Amber Addison and Ashley Dewitt. They were also Miley's and Lilly's archenemies. But now it looked as if they were Lilly's best friends. Even odder was the way Lilly was dressed. She was wearing coordinated clothes and makeup instead of her usual skater-girl clothes. But her appearance wasn't all that had changed.

"Okay, everyone," Amber said.

"Prepare to be jealous," Lilly added.

"Because we look . . ." Ashley said.

". . . fabulous!" all three girls shouted at once. They touched their index fingers together, and made a hissing sound, as if they were sizzling hot. *"Ooooo!"*

"Noooooo!" Miley shouted. She couldn't take it. This wasn't her Lilly. Her scream drew the attention of everyone on the beach.

"Oh, you've done it now," Roxy warned.

"It's Hannah Montana!" Lilly screamed.

Everyone on the beach suddenly seemed crazed. They rushed toward Miley and Roxy, screaming for Hannah Montana.

"Angel, help!" Miley shouted.

"Freeze!" Roxy shouted as she threw her arms out.

Everyone froze. It was as if the angel had made time stop. Even Lilly was stuck in position, her arms stretched toward Hannah Montana.

"Okay, I don't want this life anymore," she told the angel. "I want to be Miley again. I want my friends back." Most of all, Miley wanted the old Lilly back.

"Too late for that," Roxy said, shaking her head. "Nobody ever gets a second wish."

"Angel, say what?"

"This is your life, *Hannah*." Roxy lowered her arm, and the people on the beach unfroze and ran toward them.

Roxy snapped her fingers again. The twinkling stars appeared and Miley vanished.

She disappeared so quickly that Lilly, Amber, and Ashley didn't realize she was gone. They kept running toward her, over the sand dune and onto the beach. But it was empty.

Chapter Four

Miley and Roxy reappeared in Hannah Montana's living room. Despite what the angel had told her, Miley was determined to go back to her previous double life, secrets and all.

"Angel, there's got to be a way to get my old life back," she said.

"I told you, superstar, only one wish per customer—no refunds or exchanges," the angel said.

Miley would have argued, but Jesse McCartney walked in just then carrying a picnic basket.

"Hey, babe," he said, kissing her on the cheek, "are you ready for our picnic on Papui?"

"What in the world is Papui?" Miley asked, wide-eyed.

"The island I bought for you," Jessie said.

"Oh, my gosh!" Maybe being Hannah all the time wasn't so bad after all. Miley turned to Roxy, amazed. "Jesse McCartney bought me an island!" she said, her voice rising with excitement.

Roxy raised an eyebrow. Miley suddenly remembered how being Hannah all the time had caused Jackson to become a hermit, Oliver to become a Rico clone, and Lilly to turn herself into a superficial fashion plate. Miley knew she couldn't go anywhere with Jesse until she had solved these problems. Not that she wasn't tempted . . .

"I'm sorry, Jesse. I can't," she said.

"Why not?"

Miley couldn't tell him the truth, not unless she wanted him to think she was completely out of her mind. "I'm sort of dealing with something right now, so . . ."

"Oh, you are so cute when you're 'dealing with something right now.'" Jesse didn't seem to mind her vague answer.

"That's sweet, Jesse, but I think I need to be alone," Miley said.

"You're so cute when you need to be alone," Jesse said, but he didn't move. He just smiled and gazed at her.

"Jesse . . ." Miley said, walking him to the door. Why wasn't this guy getting the hint?

"You're so cute when you say 'Jesse,'" he said, grinning.

Okay, that was it. Miley pushed him out the door. "Get out," she said, annoyed.

"You're so cute when you're kicking me out," Jesse said as he looked back.

"I'm serious!" Miley yelled. She slammed the door in his face. Clearly, Hannah Montana had a harder time getting rid of her boyfriends than Miley had getting them in the first place.

"Ow." Then Jesse pressed his nose up against the windowpane. "Still so cute."

Miley turned her back on him and marched over to Roxy. "Angel, there has got to be some kind of loophole."

"Well, you could . . ." Roxy thought for a minute and then shook her head. "No. Well, how about if you—no." She began to pace across the living room, trying to come up with an answer. "Oh, how about—" Finally, Roxy stopped pacing and shrugged. "Girl, I got nothing," she admitted.

"Well, I want my family back. I want my friends back. And Miley Stewart does not take 'no' for an answer!" Miley said.

"That's because Miley Stewart doesn't exist," Roxy said.

Then Miley had a brilliant idea. If Miley Stewart didn't exist, then she would bring her to life. "Not yet!" she told the angel. "But you'd be surprised what this girl can do with a wig!"

Chapter Five

After her conversation with the angel, Miley put her plan into action. She found a brown, curly wig that transformed her from Hannah Montana into Miley Stewart. Then she changed out of Hannah's pop-star clothes into the most average outfit she could find, and she headed toward the beach.

Oliver and Rico were still at the snack shop in their matching outfits. They stood near a big, metal trash can—and a telescope that was aimed at Hannah's house.

"Get your genuine Hannah Montana trash," Rico rapped. "We stole it ourselves, and we sell it for cash!"

Oliver took over. "I've got toenail clippings, and that's no hype. Clone your own Hannah while the DNA's ripe!"

"I said, what? I said, what? I said, what? I said, what?" They rapped the refrain together while they danced.

Rico looked impressed by his business partner. He bowed and kissed Oliver's ring, as if Oliver were a king.

"Respect!" the boys shouted out together.

Miley noticed that Lilly was still at the beach, too, but she was ignoring the guys and their rap act. Lilly and her friends seemed to think they were too cool to notice guys like Oliver and Rico. Miley realized that without her, Lilly and Oliver had never become friends.

Lilly, Amber, and Ashley were busy criticizing the fashion choices of everyone who walked by.

"I mean, where did she find that outfit?" Amber asked, watching a girl leave the snack bar. "Ugly-R-Us?"

"More like Ugly-R-Her!" Lilly said.

All three girls laughed.

"We are so funny," Ashley said.

"And pretty," Amber added as she flipped her long brown hair over her shoulder.

"I love us!" Lilly agreed. Just then, her watch alarm beeped.

"Time to hydrate," the girls said at the same time. They touched their index fingers together. *"Sssssss!"*

Lilly strutted over to the snack bar,

where Miley was sitting on a stool. Miley had been waiting for an opportunity to talk to her best friend alone.

"Hi," Miley said, standing up.

"Yeah, whatever," Lilly said. "Three bottled waters with lime," she said to the guy behind the counter. "Pronto."

Miley was sure that the *real* Lilly, the tomboy who loved her skateboard and who would never sit around making fun of people, was in there somewhere. "*Aaaaanyway*, I'm Miley, and I'm new here, and I was just wondering, do you want to be friends?"

"Okay, first, Miley is a stupid name," Lilly said, glaring at her. "B, I've already got friends. And *quattro*, why don't you go back to the trailer park, unhitch, and drive away?" Then Lilly turned her back to Miley and began to leave.

Miley ignored Lilly's insults, however,

and stepped in front of her. "No, no, no," she said, still determined to get through to the real Lilly. "I don't drive, but I do *skateboard*. Do you skateboard?"

Lilly laughed. "As if! It's stupid, it's sweaty, and hello?" she said, tossing her blond hair. "Who wants helmet hair?"

"You do!" Miley said. "You used to love helmet hair. And scabby knees, and elbow-pad rash! Doesn't that sound like fun?"

Lilly backed away. She seemed to be getting a little scared. Plus, if Amber and Ashley saw Lilly talking to plain old Miley, she could lose her popular-girl status. "I took a pretty girl's karate class," she warned, raising her hands and threatening to give Miley a karate chop. She turned and headed back toward her friends, completely forgetting about the water she'd ordered.

Miley stopped her. "What happened to you? You're not like this. How can you be friends with Amber and Ashley? C'mon, Lilly," she pleaded. "You're better than that."

"Okay, how do you know my name?" Lilly demanded, looking freaked out. "Oh, wait, everybody knows my name, because I'm *pop*-u-lar."

"Yeah, but does everybody know you have a birthmark shaped like a poodle on your butt?" Miley asked with her hands on her hips.

Lilly gasped. "How do you know that?" she whispered.

"Because I'm your best friend. And I know somewhere deep down inside of you, our friendship is still there," Miley said.

Lilly stared at Miley as if she were crazy.

"C'mon, look at me. Really look at me,"

Miley pleaded. "Come on, Lilly, don't you know me?"

Lilly stared at Miley. Then her eyes widened with recognition. "Oh, my gosh!"

"Yes! I knew you'd be able to see the real me!" Miley said, taking Lilly's hands.

"Of course I can! The blond hair's coming out of the wig! You're Hannah Montana!" Lilly squealed.

Lilly pulled off Miley's wig, revealing her long, blond Hannah Montana hair.

Miley couldn't believe it. She hadn't gotten through to Lilly at all. Deep down, Lilly had no idea who Miley Stewart was. Roxy was right: Miley Stewart never existed. But Hannah Montana did.

"Look everybody! Hannah Montana's back, and she knows what's on my butt!" Lilly shouted. Lilly's face dropped as she realized she had just yelled about her butt to everybody on the beach. "I can't believe I said that out loud," she said quietly.

But no one really noticed. They were too focused on the pop star in front of them. The crowd rushed over to Hannah, screaming for autographs. Camera flash-bulbs went off, blinding Miley.

"Over here, Hannah!" Oliver yelled, holding up a camera. "Smile!"

But Miley didn't see anything to smile about. None of her friends knew her—at least not as Miley.

"Come on, baby," Oliver continued. "Give me a little something-something."

Miley ran away, wishing that she could snap her fingers like Roxy and disappear.

When Miley got home, Candice was on the couch talking on her cell phone. At least her father was happy in this new life, Miley thought.

Candice held out her hand and admired a large diamond ring that glittered on one of her fingers. She was too busy marveling at her jewelry to notice that her stepdaughter had just walked in the door.

"You can't believe what he bought me!" Candice said into the telephone. "Marrying that dumb hillbilly was the smartest thing I ever did."

Dumb hillbilly? Miley couldn't believe it. Her wish had ruined everything—Jackson was a crazy hermit, Lilly was a superficial fashion queen, Oliver was selling Hannah "souvenirs," and a horrible, money-hungry woman was using her father. This was a disaster! And it was all her fault.

Chapter Six

A couple of hours later, Miley heard a knock on her bedroom door. She was under the covers, with her head at the foot of the bed. Her life was suddenly so upside down that she felt better sleeping that way.

Her father came into the room, carrying two mugs of hot chocolate. "Hey, darlin', you okay?" he asked. "You've been in here for hours."

"No," Miley said. Then she ducked under the covers again.

"Oh, boy, back-ways 'round," Mr. Stewart said. "This may be more than my *loco* hot cocoa can cure."

Loco hot cocoa? Miley came out from under the covers again. "You still make your crazy *loco* hot cocoa?"

"Of course I do. Why would you even ask a silly question like that?" Mr. Stewart said, sitting next to her on the bed.

"Because everything's wrong. Lilly and Oliver aren't my friends—"

"Who?" asked Mr. Stewart.

That just proved Miley's point. "See? And Jackson moved out—"

Her father cut her off. "No, no, no. Now that was his choice."

"Yeah, but it wouldn't have been his choice if I hadn't made that stupid wish and changed everything."

"What wish?" her father asked. "Bud, you're starting to sound more *loco* than the cocoa."

"Bud" was what Mr. Stewart called Miley. It didn't sound right now that she was all Hannah all the time. "Don't you '*bud*' me!" Miley jumped up and walked across the room. "You're the one who married a blood-sucking leech who doesn't even love you!"

"Aha! So that's what this is all about," Mr. Stewart said. "Your stepmama warned me you might resent her a little bit. She's so smart about teenage girls."

"That's because last year she *was* one," Miley muttered.

"Now you hold on there, young lady. I understand your being upset, but one thing that will never change is you and me and our *loco* hot cocoa." Mr. Stewart clinked his mug against Miley's and took a sip. He ended up with a whipped-cream mustache.

Just then, Candice poked her head into the room. "Oh, there you are. Hey, I was wondering—"

Miley rolled her eyes.

Candice stopped short when she saw what Mr. Stewart was holding. "Oh, snap! Is that hot chocolate? *Eeewww!* Get it out! Get it out! I'm horribly allergic. I get massive, massive headaches!"

Mr. Stewart merely stared at her.

"And you know what I am like when I get my headaches," she continued.

Mr. Stewart grabbed the mug out of Miley's hand and headed for the bedroom door. "*Adios, loco* cocoa."

"But, Daddy, what about our special drink?" Miley asked.

"Oh, just drink some tea. What's the big

deal?" Candice said. "Whiny little baby," she added under her breath as she followed Mr. Stewart out the door. "Robby! Candy needs a shopping spree to make her head feel better!" she said sweetly. She looked over her shoulder at Miley and smiled, then slammed the door behind her.

Miley grabbed a pillow and threw it across the room. It hit the wall and landed on a jewelry box with a Hannah Montana logo. The box opened, and a tiny Hannah Montana doll popped up and began singing.

"Oh, shut it," Miley snapped. She wanted her old life back. She walked out on the balcony outside her room.

She sank into a chair, completely bummed. "Oh, Miley, why did you ever make that stupid wish?" she asked herself. "I hate my life!"

"I ain't so crazy about it either."

Miley jumped. She hadn't been expecting

an answer. However, Jackson was sitting on the roof next to a little television.

"Jackson, you came back!" Miley said.

"Well, you're darn tootin'! I may be a grumpy hermit, but I still need my reality TV," Jackson said. "Now quiet, Chauntel's about ready to eat a bug!"

"Jackson, it's just us. You don't have to do the voice," Miley said.

"What voice? Oh, right," Jackson said, switching to his normal tone. "Sometimes I forget."

"Oh, you know what? I don't care about the voice. I'm just so happy you came back!" Miley decided she could ignore the long, tangled hair, the scraggly beard, and the distinctive odor. She reached to give her brother a big hug. "Welcome home!"

Jackson pulled away. "Wow. Did you hear me? I'm not staying."

"But, Jackson, you have to!" Miley realized how much she had missed him, along with everything else that she'd taken for granted and lost when she made her stupid wish. "I want at least some of my old life back. I mean, you and I weren't perfect, and we fought, but we loved each other, and Dad loved us, and there was no evil stepmom, and I had great friends, and it was all because the world didn't know I was Hannah Montana."

"A world that didn't know you were Hannah Montana. I'd wish for that any day," Jackson said.

The second the words were out of Jackson's mouth, a shooting star flashed across the sky.

Miley realized she might have only one wish, but didn't that mean Jackson had a wish, too? "Angel! Angel!" Miley called.

"A shooting star! A shooting star! Right when he wished! Come on! That's got to count for something. Please?" Miley waited. Nothing happened. "Oh, man, I'm stuck like this forever."

Miley tugged at her hair in frustration, wishing it were brown. To her surprise, the blond wig came off. Miley's hair was her own again. Long, brown, and curly.

Suddenly, Jackson disappeared, and there were twinkling stars left in his place. The angel who looked like Roxy appeared. "Congratulations," she said.

Just then, thunder boomed, and Roxy looked up at the sky. "What? She found a loophole." She turned to Miley and smiled. "You have yourself a wonderful life, Miley," she said, then snapped her fingers and disappeared.

The next thing Miley knew, she was back

on the porch with Lilly, leaning on the railing. It was as if Miley had never made her wish.

Lilly stood next to her, gazing at the sky. "*Oooh*, look. A shooting star. I wish for an A on the project. What do you wish for?"

Miley looked at Lilly, who didn't mind skinned knees or skateboarder's elbow-pad rash or touching worms. If Lilly was back to normal, then everything else would be, too. Miley realized that her life was perfect just the way it was, even if it led to some confusion now and then.

"I don't wish for anything. I love my life exactly the way it is," Miley said, pulling Lilly into a hug.

Lilly gave her friend a confused look. She didn't know what had made Miley so sentimental all of a sudden, but Lilly didn't care. Miley was her best friend, and Lilly hugged her back.

Part One

Supercute, supertalented Jesse McCartney was in Hannah's dressing room!

"I wish I was just Hannah Montana all the time. It sure would make life a whole lot easier," Miley said.

"What is going on?!" Miley yelled.

"You wished for one life, and you got it," Roxy explained. "In this world, Miley Stewart never existed."

"The perfect night with the perfect girl!" Jesse said, gazing into Miley's eyes.

Rico was wearing the same outfit as Oliver.

It was as if the angel had made time stop. Lilly was stuck, her arms stretched toward Hannah Montana.

"I don't wish for anything. I love my life exactly the way it is," Miley said, pulling Lilly into a hug.

Part Two

"My job is to protect Hannah Montana from danger. *All* kinds of danger," Roxy said, giving Jeremy a stern look.

Miley collapsed onto the couch. "Dad, this night was a disaster."

"*Ooh*, sushi! President likey," said the president
of the United States.

The president was impressed with Hannah's
imitation of him.

Mr. Stewart was looking for a disguise to wear as
Hannah's manager.

"I thought teaching America's angel one of my songs
would be a great way to serve my country,"
Hannah said.

Miley knelt next to Humphrey's chair. "I guess I'll just whisper to the dog."

Roxy yanked him back into their hug. "I'm not done. Two whole days, Robby Ray!"

PART TWO

Chapter One

Miley Stewart danced down the hall outside her dressing room. She and her backup dancers had just tried out some new moves for a special concert. Rehearsal was over, but Miley had had so much fun that she didn't want to stop dancing!

"Great rehearsal, guys," she said, still in her Hannah Montana wig and outfit.

The dancers all thanked her.

"I can't believe we're actually going to be

performing for the president of the United States," said Jeremy, a new addition to the group. Carried away by his enthusiasm, he took hold of Miley's arms and gave her a squeeze. "That is *so* cool!"

Miley stepped back, and all the other dancers gasped.

"Did you see that? The new guy touched me!" Miley said. "Didn't anybody tell him? Hello! Never touch the star. Never, ever, ever!" she yelled, snapping her fingers in Jeremy's face.

"Oh . . . uh . . . I . . ." Jeremy tried to apologize, but he was too stunned to speak.

"Gotcha!" Miley said with a big smile.

The other dancers laughed and high-fived each other before heading to their dressing rooms. Jeremy was still so surprised he hadn't moved.

"We do that to all the new dancers,"

Miley said. "I hope you're not mad at me."

"Mad? Try totally humiliated," Jeremy said, then started to walk away. "I am so out of here!" he yelled.

"Jeremy!" Miley called. She didn't want to lose him. In addition to being a great dancer, Jeremy was both cute and nice.

He turned around, smiling. "Gotcha back!"

"*Oooh*, you're good," she said. She had completely believed him.

"Good enough to go to a movie with tonight?" Jeremy asked.

"I'd like that," Miley said, smiling shyly.

Suddenly, Roxy barreled out of Hannah Montana's dressing room. She was Hannah's bodyguard, and she took her job very seriously. "Me, too!" she told Jeremy. "I'm in the mood for a comedy. Or maybe something where Taye Diggs takes his shirt off. Either one works for me."

Miley rolled her eyes. Roxy was always on the alert when it came to protecting Hannah Montana. "Jeremy," she said, frustrated, "this is my bodyguard, Roxy."

Roxy stepped between Miley and Jeremy, giving him the once-over. Then she linked arms with each of them, making sure she stayed in the middle. "That's right. And my job is to protect Hannah Montana from danger. *All* kinds of danger," she said, giving Jeremy a stern look. "Know what I'm saying, dancer boy?"

Jeremy nodded, but he didn't seem to know what to say.

"I think you do," Roxy continued. She smiled, but her eyes were all business.

When Miley got home later that night, she was still wearing her Hannah Montana wig and clothes.

Her father was making a smoothie. "So how was the date?" he asked.

"Mine or hers?" Miley said grumpily.

Roxy walked in holding a big tub of popcorn. "Free refills, and Taye took his shirt off twice. I'd give it two thumbs-up, but I don't want to let go of my bucket."

"Daddy, he's never going to ask me out again," Miley complained.

"Oh, honey, you say that about every boy you and Roxy date," Mr. Stewart teased.

"Hello? Do I even have to tell you what's wrong with that sentence?" Miley asked. The boys who asked out Hannah Montana didn't exactly plan on being accompanied by a martial-arts expert who watched their every move.

"Sense of humor! That'll help you later in life," Roxy said with a laugh. "Now, you're singing for the president tomorrow. You need to get your rest, and I need to go home and find my bulletproof panty hose."

Miley and her father looked at each other. Was there such a thing as bulletproof panty hose? Miley wondered.

"Keeps bullets out; keeps Roxy in," the bodyguard said on her way to the door.

Miley watched her leave. "Dad, this night was a disaster."

"Oh, I'm sure it wasn't that bad," Mr. Stewart said, sitting down next to her. "I bet the boy had a good time."

"Dad, Roxy put a bell around his arm. So every time he tried to make a move, it went *ding, ding, ding, ding*!" She threw her arm around her father's shoulders to demonstrate.

"Exactly how many times did that boy ding?" Mr. Stewart asked.

"It doesn't matter, Daddy. Every time he went *ding*, she went, 'don't'. And I went *dang*!"

"Well, honey, Roxy's just doing her job. And to be honest with you, I agree with her. 'Cause when it comes to girls, boys'll say and do just about anything."

As if to prove his father's point, Jackson walked down the stairs and into the kitchen, talking on his cell phone.

"No, no, Julie," he said. "I'm serious. I'm a professional motocross racer."

Miley and her father stopped to listen. The closest Jackson had ever gotten to a motocross race was watching one on TV.

"Heck, yeah! I'm working on my bike right now," Jackson said into the phone. He turned on the blender, pushing buttons to make it sound like he was revving up a motocross bike.

"Listen to that engine purr," he said. "Julie? Julie?" He turned off the blender. Julie had hung up. "Aw, man, how could she not believe me?" he asked.

"I'm guessing you pureed when you should have liquefied," his father teased.

"Of course!" Jackson said, hitting himself on the forehead. He raced upstairs to come up with a new plan.

Miley watched him go, shaking her head. "Dad, not all boys are like that. I bet you didn't lie to girls."

"Well, honey, when you got a head of hair like this, you don't have to," Mr. Stewart said, running his hand through his hair.

Miley rolled her eyes. If her father had anything to say about it, she definitely wasn't going to get rid of the third wheel on her dates anytime soon.

Or would she?

Chapter Two

The next night, Hannah Montana performed for a sold-out crowd—one that included the president of the United States and his daughter, Sophie Martinez.

After the show, Miley and Lilly followed Roxy back to the dressing room. It was decorated in red, white, and blue for President Martinez's visit. Lilly had dressed for the occasion. She was disguised as Lola Luftnagle, Hannah's best friend.

Tonight she was wearing a red, white, and blue outfit and a red wig.

A Secret Service agent in a dark suit and sunglasses stood at the door. "I have a visual on Montana. Repeat, I have a visual on Montana," he said into a small microphone on his wrist. "Yes, I'll get her autograph, Mom. Love you, too." Then he switched to a mic on his other wrist. "Bring in the president."

"Wow, the president!" Lilly said. Then she spotted the buffet. "*Ooh*, sushi. Lola likey." She snagged a salmon roll while they waited for the president to arrive.

Mr. Stewart, disguised as Hannah's manager, opened the door and walked in. He was followed by President Martinez and his daughter.

"Mr. President, Sophie, I'd like you to meet Hannah Montana," said Mr. Stewart.

The Secret Service agent stepped forward. "Hold, please," he said to Sophie. Then he put his hands over the president's ears. "And go."

Sophie, a huge Hannah Montana fan, let out a high-pitched scream.

Miley and everyone else in the room covered their ears.

"I can't believe I'm meeting Hannah Montana!" Sophie finally said, throwing her arms around Miley.

"I can't believe I'm meeting America's angel," Miley replied.

"As the leader of the free world, may I say your concert was off the hook, and you were da bomb," said President Martinez.

Miley looked at Lilly. Had the president really just said she was "da bomb"?

"Daddy, keep it real or keep it quiet," Sophie whispered.

"What? Just because I live in the White *Hizzle* doesn't mean I got no sizzle," said the president.

Sophie cringed, looking mortified.

"Don't worry, sweetie," Miley told her. "All dads are embarrassing."

"Yeah, but yours never stopped a motorcade because he saw a horsey," Sophie replied.

"Now, Sophie, horses have owners and owners vote," President Martinez said. Then he turned to Mr. Stewart. "And I got to feed him a carrot!"

"Oh, don't you love it when those big, fat, hairy lips tickle the palm of your hand?" asked Mr. Stewart.

Suddenly it was Miley's turn to feel embarrassed. Her father was talking to the president about horse lips.

"That's my favorite part," President Martinez said, nodding in agreement. Then he noticed the buffet table. "*Ooh*, sushi! President likey," he said. "Watch this." He picked up a tuna roll. "The Japanese ambassador loves this."

Roxy sniffed the air. Something wasn't right. In fact, something was very, very wrong. That sushi had been sitting out for too long!

The president tossed the sushi into the air, then opened his mouth to catch it.

Roxy dove across the room. As the piece of tuna roll was about to land in the president's mouth, Roxy grabbed it, accidentally knocking him over. He fell into three Secret Service agents, and Roxy landed on the floor.

Miley had thought she was embarrassed before. Now she was completely mortified. Her bodyguard had just tackled the president of the United States.

"Roxy, what are you doing?" Miley asked as she rushed over.

"Really, there's enough for everyone," the president said.

"Enough to get you sick," Roxy explained. She held up the piece of sushi. "Sorry, sir, but what you've got here is a case of fish gone funky!"

"Excuse me?" said President Martinez, frowning.

Suddenly, Lilly clutched her stomach. "Oh, boy, the salmon's coming back upstream," she shouted, then dashed toward the bathroom.

Roxy was right. The fish *was* funky.

"Amazing," the president said. "A nose like that should be working for the president of the United States."

"I'm honored, sir, but I can't leave Hannah," said Roxy.

"Yes, you can!" Miley said quickly. If Roxy became the president's bodyguard instead of Hannah's, Miley could go on dates without Roxy and her bells.

"What?" Roxy said, shocked. She loved protecting Hannah Montana. Miley and her family had become Roxy's family, too. Why would Miley want her to go?

Miley realized she had sounded a bit too eager to see Roxy leave her for another job. "I mean," she stammered, "you cannot pass up an opportunity like this. He's the . . ." She deepened her voice and imitated President Martinez. ". . . president of the United States."

The president was impressed. "Not bad! Up top, Ms. Montana!" he said, raising his hand for a high five.

"Up top, Mr. Prez," Miley said, and high-fived the president.

Roxy had not been convinced about accepting the president's job offer. When they arrived home later that evening, Miley was still trying to change her mind.

"But, Roxy, your country needs your keen sense of smell," Miley argued. "I mean, sour milk, bad bologna." She pointed to Roxy's nose. "This honker's the only thing that can keep your president on the job and off the john!"

"I can appreciate that, but I still don't think that I should, you know—" Roxy stopped in midsentence when she saw Jackson carefully making his way down the stairs. He was wearing a colorful motocross outfit with bright red leather boots and carrying a red helmet. The suit was so tight that Jackson couldn't bend his arms or knees. With each step, the new leather made a squeaky noise.

"Eeee, doggies," said Mr. Stewart, trying not to laugh. "That's a nice outfit, son. I haven't seen that much leather since your grandmother got all gussied up for singles' bingo."

Jackson pretended to be amused. "Oh, ho, ho, ho, ho! Oh, Dad. Now, if you'll excuse me, I'm on my way to Julie's to tell her I took fourth place in the big race."

"Well, why not just tell her you won?" Mr. Stewart asked.

"Because this way, I don't even need to show her a trophy. Always thinking," Jackson said. He put on the helmet, gave it a tap, and closed the visor. But he didn't realize that it was nighttime and that he wouldn't be able to see through the tinted plastic. He started to leave and walked right into the door.

"You see, Miley?" Roxy said. "If I take that job, who's going to protect you from boys who are 'always thinking'? I mean, I've had your back ever since we met down at Wig City."

Miley thought back, remembering that day at Wig City a few years before. She and her dad had gone to the store looking for disguises.

The first wig Miley had tried on was long, blond, and curly. She looked in the mirror and hardly recognized herself. The blond hair was so curly, it barely fit in the mirror. It would certainly get Hannah noticed, Miley thought.

Just then, the store's security guard, Roxy, walked by. "No, no, no, no, no," she said, laughing at Miley's wig.

Miley shrugged and took it off. She picked up a spiky, black hairdo that looked very edgy and rock and roll.

Roxy walked by again. "I don't think so," she said firmly.

Miley stared after her. Who was this woman, and why did she keep disagreeing with Miley's choices? But she tried on another wig. This one had long black dreadlocks. Miley was sure it was super-cool. This was the hair that would get Hannah Montana's picture on magazine covers and help her newly recorded album rise to the top of the pop charts.

Then Roxy walked over. "All right, this is getting to be downright painful." She pulled the wig off Miley's head. "I'll be right back."

A moment later, the security guard was back, holding a long, straight-haired blond wig. She placed it on Miley's head and stepped back to take a look. "Now we're cooking with gas," Roxy said with a satisfied smile.

Miley looked in the mirror. The wig was perfect! It had instantly transformed Miley into Hannah Montana, pop star! "I love it!" she said.

Mr. Stewart walked over wearing a large handlebar mustache and a blond, curly wig. He was looking for a disguise to wear as Hannah Montana's manager.

"Hey, Miley. What do you think of this one?" he asked.

Roxy took one look at him and realized her job wasn't done. "I'm guessing you're the daddy," she said. Then she turned to Miley. "Don't worry, I'll help him next."

Roxy grabbed his wig and walked away to search for a better one.

That was the day Roxy had become Hannah's bodyguard and friend. She'd had Miley's back ever since.

Miley shook her head, and the memory disappeared. Roxy was standing in front of her, waiting for a reply. Roxy was the best bodyguard Hannah Montana could ever ask for, but she was also cramping Miley's social life. It was time for her to be able to go on dates without a chaperone, Miley decided.

"I know, and you've changed my life, too. But let's face it, Roxy," Miley said, pointing to her bodyguard's nose. "This *schnoz* is bigger than the both of us."

Roxy stepped back and narrowed her eyes. "You want me to go, don't you?" she asked.

"No, I don't," Miley lied. She looked around the room, at anything but Roxy.

"Yes, you do," Roxy said. "Because I'm all up in your boy business. Look me in the eye and tell me that isn't true."

"Okay, fine. It is!" Miley admitted. "I'm a girl. I have needs!"

"Please tell me you just said you're a girl who has knees!" Mr. Stewart yelled from the kitchen. He didn't like the idea of his daughter dating boys any more than Roxy did.

Miley ignored him. "Roxy, it's not that I want you to go. I don't," she explained. "I just need a little space."

"Oh, sure. I give you a little space and something happens to you," Roxy said, annoyed. "That's not the way Roxy rolls."

"Well, I'm tired of Roxy rolling all over my life!" Miley yelled.

Mr. Stewart walked in from the kitchen. He tried to lighten the discussion between his daughter and the bodyguard who had become such an important part of their family. "Hey, speaking of rolls, why don't I heat up some sweet ones?" he said. "And then we can get all buttered up, and we'll sit back and be reasonable about this."

Roxy shook her head. She didn't let anyone tell her how to do her job. "I don't need to be reasonable. I just need to protect Hannah Montana. And if I can't do it full-out Roxy, I can't do it at all."

"Well, then maybe you shouldn't," Miley blurted out.

Roxy looked stunned. "Well, if that's the way you want it, then I'm happy to oblige. Good-bye, Ms. Montana," she said, heading toward the door.

Miley watched Roxy leave and then collapsed on the couch. She hadn't wanted to hurt Roxy's feelings, but life would definitely be easier now. She'd be able to go on dates without Roxy tagging along.

"I blame myself," Mr. Stewart said with a sigh as he sat down on the couch across from Miley. "I should have offered up my sticky buns sooner."

"It's not your fault, Daddy. We'll find a bodyguard better than Roxy. One who understands my—" Miley noticed that her father was glaring at her. She quickly changed what she was going to say. "—knees." She lifted her feet up off the floor and tapped her knees. "These babies right here."

Mr. Stewart didn't look convinced, but Miley was determined to prove that she was right.

Chapter Three

A few days later, Miley, disguised as Hannah Montana, and her father started to interview bodyguard candidates. One of the first was a tall, superstrong wrestler. He looked as if he could take on any over-enthusiastic fan—or all of them at once.

"So tell us something about yourself and what qualifies you to be Hannah Montana's bodyguard?" Mr. Stewart asked. He was dressed up like Hannah's manager.

"I love your music! I love what you stand for! Youth, innocence, and fun!" the wrestler shouted. He counted the reasons on his huge fingers.

Miley wondered if he thought he needed to be heard all over the building. She was just two feet away, and *that* was beginning to seem too close.

"And if anybody threatens that, I'll rip their guts out and feed them to the pigeons!" the wrestler added.

Miley and Mr. Stewart stared at him, openmouthed. Was this guy putting on a performance, or was he for real?

The wrestler flexed his enormous muscles. For a second Miley thought he might rip *her* guts out. Miley suddenly thought of Roxy. She imagined Roxy wearing the wrestler's clothes and speaking in his voice.

"I'm the bodyguard you want," Roxy shouted in Miley's vision. "I'm the bodyguard you need! *Grrrrr!*" Roxy gritted her teeth and flexed her arms.

Miley shook her head, and the vision of Roxy disappeared. She realized that the wrestler was still standing in front of her. "Thank you, Mister . . ." She checked his resume for his name. ". . . Annihilator." She watched with relief as he left the room.

The next applicant wore a sombrero, an old poncho over a denim shirt, and a bandanna tied around his neck. "There's a lot of bad *hombres* out there looking to pump up the party," he said. "Well, I got one question for 'em."

Miley clearly had Roxy on the brain, because she suddenly imagined Roxy dressed in this applicant's clothes, too.

"You got nerve?" Miley envisioned Roxy

asking. "Well, do ya, punk? Do ya?"

Miley shook her head, and Roxy disappeared again. The cowboy stood in front of her looking quite threatening. "Thank you, Mister . . . Mysterious Stranger," Miley said, reading his resume. "Well, that fits," she said to her father. The guy was certainly mysterious.

The applicants for the bodyguard job seemed to get worse and worse as the day went on. One guy looked as if he had just stepped out of a movie about organized crime.

"Let me make one thing abundantly clear, princess. Anybody comes within spitting distance of you, we're gonna have to go for a little ride and maybe have a little conversation. *Capish*?" he asked.

Miley nodded. Somehow she didn't think a little conversation was really what this guy had in mind. But she was afraid to ask any questions.

The man went on. "And what I'm gonna say is—"

Just like the others, this applicant suddenly seemed to turn into Roxy before Miley's eyes.

"—*badda bing, badda boom*. End of story. *Fuggedaboutit*."

Okay, this one was the scariest bodyguard yet, but Miley wasn't sure what was making her more nervous—the bodyguards, or that each one kept turning into Roxy in her mind. She moved a little closer to Mr. Stewart. "Thank you, Mister . . ." Miley checked his resume. "There's no name here," she said finally.

"You don't need to know my name," he said.

Mr. Stewart watched him leave, then got

to his feet. "Well, Miley, you've seen more than thirty bodyguards. There must be one you like."

"There is," Miley confessed. "And I kept seeing her in every one that came in."

"You miss Roxy, don't you?"

"Yes. I made a mistake, Dad." Miley dropped the pile of resumes onto the couch. Not one of them measured up to Roxy. "I mean, sometimes she gets on my last nerve, but she's family."

"Well, the president doesn't leave town till tomorrow," Mr. Stewart said. "So you've got some time to go to the hotel and talk to her."

"C'mon, Dad," Miley said. She remembered the hurt look on Roxy's face when Miley had admitted she wanted the bodyguard to leave. "She's never going to come back after the things I said."

"You never know till you try, bud," said Mr. Stewart.

Then it wasn't just bodyguards who Miley imagined as Roxy. Suddenly, her father looked like her, too. "Stranger things have happened," Roxy said in Mr. Stewart's voice.

Miley shook her head and tried to ignore the vision. Talk about strange. "You've got that right," she said.

Meanwhile, Jackson had problems of his own. He was still trying to convince Julie that he was a motocross champion. He limped after her on the beach. "Come on, Julie, I swear," he pleaded. "I would have shown you the bike, but I crashed it. See, here are the handlebars."

He held up a bent handlebar, but Julie didn't believe him. He didn't look as if he

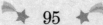

could even sit down in that tight leather uniform, let alone ride a bike. She waved Jackson away and kept walking.

Jackson tried to chase after her, but his extremely tight suit slowed him down. "Oh, c'mon, girl, don't walk so fast! I'm getting a thigh rash."

Julie walked faster.

"Oh, man," Jackson moaned. He hobbled over to Rico's Surf Shop. "Rico, do a dude a favor. Run down to the store and get me some baby powder?" he asked.

Rico looked at Jackson's suit and his pained expression. "Jackson, I say this because I care," he said seriously. "You're pathetic!"

Jackson had to admit that things with Julie hadn't gone quite as he had hoped. He'd have to come up with another plan. . . .

Chapter Four

Miley and Lilly, dressed as Hannah Montana and her friend Lola, walked into Sophie Martinez's suite at a downtown hotel. Roxy wouldn't take Miley's phone calls, so Miley had followed her father's advice and found a way to see her in person.

Agent Kaplan, the Secret Service agent assigned to protect Sophie, escorted them. "The first daughter was so excited when you called," the agent said.

"Well, I thought teaching America's angel one of my songs would be a great way to serve my country," Miley told him.

"She's such a giver," Lilly added.

Of course, it was all part of Miley's plan to find Roxy and get her to agree to come back home, but Agent Kaplan didn't know that.

"Sophie will be here momentarily," he said. "Until then, you have permission to play with the dolls. It's a lot of fun."

Miley noticed that Sophie had a table set for a tea party, with dolls and teddy bears in each of the chairs. Miley looked at Agent Kaplan. He didn't look like the tea-party type.

"So I've been told," Agent Kaplan added.

"*Oooookay*," Miley said slowly. "While I'm waiting, I think I'm just going to go say hi to one of my old bodyguards." She headed toward the door.

Agent Kaplan blocked her way. "That's a negative."

"Are you sure?" Miley asked.

"That's a positive. I have orders to keep Hannah Montana in this room. Orders from a seven-year-old." The agent made it clear that he resented being bossed around by a child, but he also had no choice. "Tomorrow we go to Make a Moose. *Wheeeee!*" he said sarcastically. Then he left the room to guard the door from the other side.

"Well, this is great," Lilly said. "Now we're stuck in here."

"No, *Hannah's* stuck in here," Miley told her. The agent had said that Hannah couldn't leave the room. He had said nothing about Lola.

"*Ohhhh,*" Lilly said, nodding.

Miley knew her friend better than that. "You don't have a clue, do you?"

"Not one," Lilly admitted.

A few minutes later, Agent Kaplan opened the door, and Sophie ran into the room wearing a Hannah Montana outfit—dark jeans, a glittering gold vest, a bright green silk jacket, and gold boots. She even wore a blond Hannah Montana wig.

"Hannah, check it out!" Sophie yelled. "I look just like you! *Woo-hoo*!"

Hannah turned around. Sophie thought her pop-star idol looked a little different, but she had no way of knowing that Hannah was actually Lilly, wearing the Hannah wig and clothes.

"Wow, you look even more like me than I do!" Lilly said with a fake Tennessee accent.

Sophie twirled to show off her entire look.

"Let's learn that new song!" Lilly said. She turned her back on Sophie and started to dance and sing. Lilly hoped that Sophie wouldn't listen too closely. Lilly couldn't sing well, and she wasn't much of a dancer.

Sophie crossed her arms and watched with a puzzled expression. This wasn't what she'd expected when she heard that Hannah Montana wanted to hang out and teach her a song. What had happened to Hannah Montana's talent?

Meanwhile, Miley had snuck out of Sophie's hotel room disguised in Lilly's red wig and funky Lola clothes. She snuck around the floor looking for Roxy. She had to be somewhere.

Miley poked her head into an important-looking room with fancy furniture. "Roxy?" she whispered. "Roxy? Roxy?"

She heard someone whistling "Hail to the Chief" and tried to back out of the room. Just then, another door opened, and the president walked into the room.

"Oh, there you are," President Martinez said. "Well, you're early."

"I am?" Miley backed toward the door. "Well, then why don't I go away and come back? Toodles!"

"Oh, no, I know how in demand you are," said the president, stopping her. "I hear you're the finest dog whisperer on the West Coast."

"Dog whisperer?" Miley asked, confused.

At that moment, a dog let out a loud howl.

"Poor Humphrey," said President Martinez, kneeling next to a brown-and-white dog lying on a chair. "He won't eat, and he looks sadder than the vice president did when he heard I passed my physical." The president rubbed the dog's belly, but Humphrey didn't move. He didn't even wag his tail. "Can you help him, please?"

Help him? Miley had no idea what to do for a sad dog. "I'd love to, but I just got an emergency call," she said, turning toward the door. "Bashful beagle in Beverly Hills. Very sad," she said, putting her hand over her heart and pretending to be upset. "Toodles!"

Miley rushed to leave, but a Secret Service agent blocked her way.

"Please," the president said. "You're my last hope. And I'm not asking as the president. I'm asking as a loving dog owner." He coughed into his hand. "Who can get you a ride on Air Force One."

Reluctantly, Miley turned around. She couldn't tell the president that she wasn't who he thought she was, or that she was sneaking around looking for Roxy.

"Yes, Mr. President," Miley said with a salute. She knelt next to Humphrey's chair. "I guess I'll just whisper to the dog," she said, lifting Humphrey's ear. "Where's Roxy?" she whispered.

"What's that?" the president asked.

"Please, let me do my job. I don't tell you how to run the country," Miley said.

"Point made. Carry on," said the president with a nod.

Humphrey started to whimper. Miley rubbed his ears and pretended to understand. "Uh-huh. Uh-huh," she said. "Yes. I'll tell him." She looked up at the president. "He's sick of his food. Kibble, kibble, kibble. Boring!"

"You're amazing!" the president said, picking up the phone. "Could I get room service? This is the president of the United States," he said into the phone. "Yes, I'll hold." He looked up and saw Miley trying to sneak out of the room. "And so will you," he told her.

Miley and the president waited for room service. Finally, a waiter delivered multiple bowls of dog food to tempt Humphrey. The dog didn't move. He looked at the food with a sad expression.

"Well, look at that. There it is. Looks delicious," Miley said. She wanted to get out of the room before the president realized she was a complete fraud. "And we're back to toodles. See ya!" she said, heading for the door.

"Whoa, whoa, whoa. Wait a second," said the president, stopping her. "He's still not eating."

"Okay, okay," Miley said with a sigh. She knelt down next to Humphrey and pretended to eat. Maybe he needed some encouragement, she thought. "*Mmmmm, Humphrey. All your favorites.*" The hotel waiter had placed menu cards behind each bowl. Miley read the cards out loud. "Boiled liver. *Mmmmm,*" she read. She tried not to look or sound as disgusted as she felt. "Ox-tongue stew. Yeah! Calf-brains fricassee. *Num, num, num.*"

Humphrey didn't even move. He ignored Miley and the food.

"I think he knows you're faking," the president said.

"You have got to be kidding me," said Miley. Eating dog food was going way too far, even to get Roxy back. Then Miley thought about how much she missed her bodyguard.

"I'd do it myself, but I just got my teeth whitened, and I can't afford a meat stain," said the president.

"I better get a medal out of this," Miley whispered to the dog. She put her face over the bowl of boiled liver. It was the least disgusting-looking item on the table. She took a bite, eating out of the bowl as if she were a dog. "*Oooh*," she said, trying not to gag. "That's some good liver." As the president watched, she gave Humphrey a thumbs-up sign. The dog ignored her. This was going to be a lot harder than Miley had expected.

Chapter Five

While Miley was trying to convince the president's dog to eat, Lilly was trying to convince the president's daughter that she was Hannah Montana. She finished the song "Nobody's Perfect" and struck a pose.

Sophie looked at her suspiciously. "Are you sure you're Hannah Montana?"

"Of course I am!" Lilly said. "Why would you ask a silly question like that?"

"Oh, I don't know. Maybe because

you stink on ice," Sophie retorted.

Lilly tried to cover. "What do you expect? I didn't bring my lights. I didn't bring my band."

"Yeah, you didn't bring your talent either," Sophie said bluntly.

Lilly gasped, pretending to be insulted.

"I just want the Hannah Montana I saw onstage," Sophie continued.

"So do I, kid. So do I," Lilly said.

At that moment, the Hannah Montana who Sophie had seen onstage was still kneeling in front of a dog-food buffet. Although Miley had eaten almost everything in front of her, Humphrey had not moved.

"C'mon, eat, puppy. Eat! I'm begging you," Miley pleaded.

"Why don't you try the brains?" the president suggested.

"If I had any," Miley muttered, "I wouldn't be here right now." She shuddered and moved closer to the bowl. She took a mouthful of the brains. Just then, she heard Roxy's voice.

"Mr. President, the dog whisperer is here," Roxy said.

"Thank you, Agent Obvious," the president said, pointing to Miley. He still thought she was the dog whisperer.

"Well, I thought she was outside—" Roxy got a look at Miley, who was kneeling on the floor next to Humphrey. Even with the red Lola wig, Roxy recognized Miley instantly. "Oh, sweet niblets!" she yelled.

Miley looked up. Her mouth and chin were covered in fricassee. "*Rut ro*," she growled.

Roxy marched over and pulled Miley to

her feet. "Mr. President, I don't know what's going on here, but I have to tell you—"

"Oh, wait!" Miley interrupted. If the president found out that she was really Miley Stewart, who was really Hannah Montana, then her secret could get out. Plus, she wanted to be able to talk to Roxy before the Secret Service threw her out— or worse, arrested her for impersonating a dog whisperer.

"Humphrey has something he wants to say," Miley insisted.

Roxy crossed her arms over her chest. "Oh, I can't wait to hear this," she said.

"What's that, Humphrey?" Miley asked, pretending to listen to the dog. "The reason you haven't been eating is . . . is because you miss somebody terribly?"

Humphrey moaned, as if he agreed.

"Well, why don't you just tell that person?" Miley asked.

Humphrey moaned again, and then gave a little bark.

"Oh, you have, but they wouldn't answer your phone calls," she said with a pointed look at Roxy. Then she remembered that this was supposed to be about Humphrey, not Miley. "I, I mean, listen to you."

"Hold on. I think I know what's going on here," the president said, nodding.

"You do?" Miley and Roxy said at the same time. Had he figured out who Miley was and why she was there?

"Of course," he answered, kneeling in front of Humphrey. "My Humphrey-mumphrey misses me. I've been so busy. I've been ignoring you, haven't I, boy?"

Humphrey wagged his tail.

"Now hold on, Mr. President," Roxy

said. "Maybe it wasn't your fault. Maybe Humphrey was being disobedient, stubborn, and a little bratty."

Miley knew exactly who Roxy was talking about, and it wasn't Humphrey. "Oh, yeah? Well, Humphrey says he was just trying to be a dog," she said. "And sometimes dogs need to be let off the leash."

"*Ahhh*," the president said, slowly.

"But what if that dog runs off and gets itself into all kinds of trouble?" Roxy asked. She didn't seem convinced.

"*Ohhh*," the president said, considering.

"Well, you have got to trust that you've trained it well enough to know right from wrong," Miley said. "And you have."

Humphrey barked and jumped up.

"What's that, buddy?" the president asked, looking at Miley for a translation.

"He said he loves you, and he knows that

you love him, too," Miley said, looking at Roxy.

Roxy smiled.

"I do. I do!" the president said. "And we're going to be spending a lot more time together, starting now."

Humphrey wagged his tail.

"C'mon, buddy. I saw a French poodle in the lobby, and she's quite the hottie," said President Martinez to his dog.

Roxy and Miley watched them leave. Both the president and Humphrey walked with a happy bounce in their steps.

"I do love you, Roxy," Miley said.

"And I love you. That's why I want to protect you," Roxy told her.

"I know, but maybe . . ." Miley sat next to Roxy on the couch.

"Maybe I do a little too much sometimes?" Roxy finished.

"Roxy, I don't want you out of my life. I just want you in it a smidge less. I know that's not the way Roxy rolls, but maybe—"

"Child, you ate dog food for me," Roxy said, cutting her off. "Maybe I can bend a little for you."

"So you're not going to come on dates with me anymore?" Miley asked with a hopeful expression.

"No," Roxy said firmly. "I'm saying you just won't see me."

"I can live with that," Miley said with a smile.

Roxy smiled, too. "So can I." She pulled Miley into a hug and then leaned back. "*Oooh*, but what I can't live with is that doggy breath. *Whoo! Stanky!*" She waved a hand under her nose and then smiled again. "But you're still cute."

Chapter Six

It didn't take Roxy long to resign from the Secret Service. The president was sorry to lose the power of her nose and its ability to smell funky fish at fifty paces, but he understood. He was so happy about Humphrey that he was willing to forgive just about anything.

Miley breezed through her front door, happier than she'd been since Roxy had left. "Hey, Daddy, look who's back," she said.

"Of course I'm back," Roxy said, as she strolled in behind her. "The president and his daughter are wonderful people, but they're not family. I was there two days and not one single hug."

Mr. Stewart stood up and opened his arms to welcome Roxy home. "Well, let me just take care of that right now. It's good to have you back." He and Roxy hugged. After a minute Mr. Stewart started to pull away.

Roxy yanked him back into their hug. "I'm not done. Two whole days, Robby Ray!"

Miley laughed. It was only then that Mr. Stewart noticed what his daughter was wearing.

"Miley, why are you dressed up like Lola?" he asked.

"Oh, right, we had to switch back at the

hotel and—" Miley stopped in midsentence and gasped. She had completely forgotten about Lilly. Her best friend was still with Sophie, impersonating Hannah Montana! "Oh, no, Lilly!" she cried.

Miley dashed out the front door. Roxy was right behind her.

Sophie Martinez had lined up her dolls and stuffed animals like an audience. She knew Hannah Montana's music videos by heart, and Lilly's dance moves were definitely not right. Sophie didn't understand what had happened to her favorite pop star, but she was determined to teach Hannah Montana her own moves.

"Now, we are going to do this until we get it right," Sophie announced firmly. "Now, one more time from the top."

"But—" Lilly said weakly. She was

panting from exhaustion. Sophie had not let up on her for one moment.

"What's that, everyone?" Sophie asked, putting her hand to her ear.

Agent Kaplan was on his knees, behind the dolls, pretending to be their voices. "Encore! Encore!" he said in a high-pitched voice. He deepened his voice, pretending to be the teddy bear. "More! More!" he growled, waving the bear's arm.

"You heard them. Now five, six, seven, eight!" Sophie counted off.

Lilly wobbled to her feet and started to dance and sing.

Agent Kaplan looked at her sympathetically.

The song was about mistakes and bad days. At the end, Lilly threw herself into a chair. "I'm having one right now," she muttered.

"At least you get to go home," Agent Kaplan said.

They both watched Sophie dance around like a choreographer. When Roxy and Miley arrived to pick up "Hannah," the first daughter was still dancing and had started singing Hannah's hit song "Nobody's Perfect."

Miley and Roxy looked at each other and smiled. It had been a crazy couple of days, and they were glad everything was back to normal . . . almost.

Put your hands together for the next Hannah Montana book . . .

One of a Kind

Adapted by Laurie McElroy

Based on the series created by Michael Poryes and Rich Correll & Barry O'Brien

Based on the episode, "I Am Hannah, Hear Me Croak," Written by Michael Poryes

Hannah Montana danced across the stage, singing the final chorus of her song "Life's What You Make It." She brought yet another powerhouse performance to an end with her strong, clear voice, and the crowd went wild, chanting, "We love you! We love you!"

"Thank you!" Hannah called out. "I love you, too!" She waved her microphone and blew kisses. "Good night, everybody!"

But her fans weren't ready to say good-bye. They started chanting her name. "Hannah! Hannah! Hannah!"

What a concert! thought Hannah. "You guys want more?" she called out. "Y'all are awesome!"

The crowd's chants grew even louder. "Hannah! Hannah!"

"I'll sing all night long if you want me to!" Hannah called back. She was having a great time. She didn't want the night to end either. She loved singing for her fans more than almost anything. After all, it's what being a pop star was all about! She turned to her band. "Let's kick it, guys!" she said.

The band played the first notes of "I Got Nerve." Then Hannah's voice filled the concert arena, and her fans went crazy enjoying another hit-filled set.

The next morning, at the family's beach house in Malibu, Jackson Stewart was thinking about his sister's concert the night before.

"*You want some toast,*" he sang, making up his own words to "I Got Nerve," as he and his dad made breakfast. "*I bet you do.*"

"*Please add some jam and but-ter, too,*" Mr. Stewart joined in.

"*We're out of grape, so sad,*" Jackson sang. "*It's all your fault, you bad dad.*"

Mr. Stewart stopped dancing. "You know what, son?" he said.

"Yeah, Dad?"

"You got nerve," Mr. Stewart teased.

Jackson laughed.

Just then, Miley Stewart appeared at the top of the stairs, bleary-eyed and still in her pajamas. Without her long, blond Hannah Montana wig and her makeup, Miley looked just like any other high-school girl. And that's exactly the way she wanted it. Only her family and closest friends knew that Miley Stewart and Hannah Montana were one and the same person. Miley loved being up onstage as Hannah. She loved singing, dancing, and rocking the house. But she loved her normal life, too.

Sometimes living a secret double life was exhausting. It was hard being a full-time high-school student and a teen superstar at the same time. As much as Miley enjoyed being Hannah, she wanted to make sure that people liked her for who she was and not because she was a pop star. So she lived her day-to-day life as average, brown-haired Miley Stewart and put on a blond wig and glittery clothes when it was time to transform herself into a pop sensation.

It was the best of both worlds, just as her hit song said.

Her dad, Robby Stewart, started applauding as soon as he saw her. "There she is. Six encores. The voice that wouldn't stop."

"Well, they were such a great audi—" Miley paused and cleared her throat. Her voice was all hoarse and scratchy. "They were such a great—" That sounded even worse. "Whoa, this isn't good," she whispered.

"Here, take a sip of this," Mr. Stewart said, handing her a glass of orange juice.

Miley drank it quickly, sure the healthy liquid would change her croaky-frog voice back into that of a pop princess. She sang a line from one of her songs, practically choking.

Jackson cringed. Now his younger sister sounded even worse.

Miley turned to her father with a panicked expression. What had happened to her voice? "Help me!" she croaked.